EVERY YEAR, Old Grey and her companions make the 10,000 kilometre journey from the wintery Arctic waters to the warmth of the Mexican sun, to breed and to have their calves. Every year, as summer comes to the Arctic, they make the journey back, to feed and grow fat. In her fifty years Old Grey, fifteen metres long and thirty-four tonnes, has swum a distance equal to travelling to the moon and home again…

Whale Journey

Written by
VIVIAN FRENCH

Illustrated by
LISA FLATHER

SEAGULLS FLY in long slow loops above
Baja California. The coastline is ragged
edged; the land
zigzags in and
out, and small
islands are
dotted all around.

In the San Ignacio lagoon, a long mottled
grey ridge, encrusted with jewel-like
barnacles, heaves up out of the sea, waves
slipping and slapping against its sides.
A young gull swoops to land, swerves,
and then soars again. This is no ridge of
hard rock – this is Old Grey.

In the lagoon the sea is warm. The sun glints and sparkles on the clear blue water, and now the gull sees two huge grey shapes circling slowly under the surface. Old Grey knows her calf will soon be born. Three Scars, another female, knows it too. She stays close to Old Grey's side, waiting for the moment when the calf begins to slide from its mother's body.

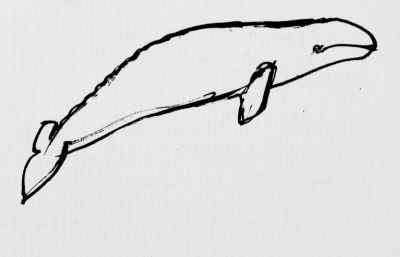

THE TWO WHALES rise to the surface together to breathe. As they blow, the spouts of air and water make rainbows in the sunshine. They dive again, and this time Old Grey moves a little further from the shore. Her calf is coming. Three Scars sees a tail emerging, and then, with a slither, he is born.

Old Grey, with a swirl, twists away to break the
umbilical cord, and Little Grey starts sinking in his
new world of light and melting shadows. Three Scars
swims beneath him, and gently, smoothly, carries him
up to the other world above. As Old Grey comes back
close beside him, he takes his first breath.

LITTLE GREY is small for a baby grey whale, maybe less than four metres long. Old Grey's other calves have been nearer five metres, but Little Grey is strong. By the evening he is pushing at Old Grey to feed from her, and he is trying to swim and dive.

Three Scars stays near. When Little Grey splashes and rolls she slides by, and the ripples of her passing set him the right way up again.

Little Grey is learning the ways of the water; the smoothness, the wetness, the boundlessness of the ocean... and he rolls again, just for the fun of it.

AT THE BEGINNING OF FEBRUARY

Little Grey is a month old. He has grown,
and is beginning to get a thicker layer
of blubber-fat under his smooth grey skin.
This will keep him warm on his long
journey north. As he travels further and
further up into the cold icy waters it will
grow thicker still.

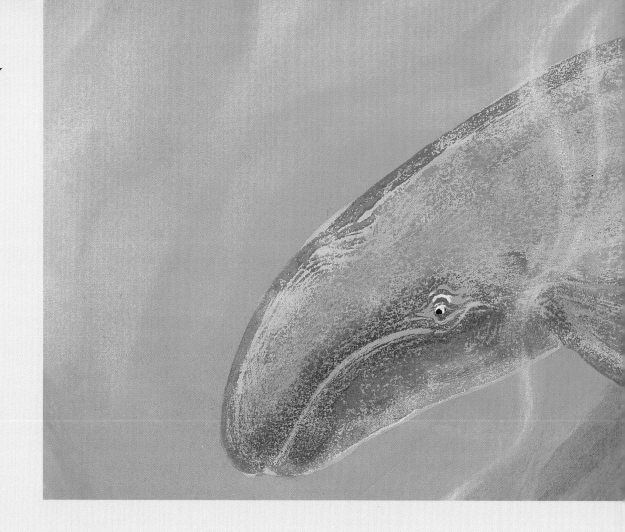

As yet, Little Grey knows nothing of journeys. His world is full of fascinating sounds and sensations. Old Grey is teaching him the language of the sea: cool water currents mean deeper water, beware a sudden swirl, watch for shadows above and below, listen, look, feel.

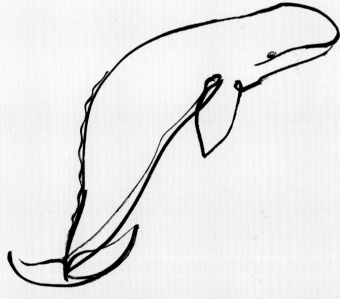

FEBRUARY COMES AND GOES. Old Grey and Little Grey swim around and about the lagoons and bays, and each day Little Grey grows stronger. Other adult grey whales are still playing and rolling in the deeper ocean waters, but each day there are fewer to be seen as they leave in twos and threes for the Arctic feeding grounds.

Even Three Scars has gone, and Little Grey can sense a strange longing deep inside Old Grey... he does not yet understand the longing but it is somewhere inside him too. He is not surprised when, at the beginning of March, Old Grey turns her back on Baja California and swims steadily north. Keeping close to her side, Little Grey begins his longest journey yet.

It is a serious business swimming to the North.
Old Grey keeps a clear rhythm as she goes –
dive, slide down through the water,
heave and thrust with her tail
to drive herself on, and then back up to
the surface to blow, four or five spouts for her
five minutes underwater. After the last blow
she dives once more and, as she dives, her tail
flukes break clear above the waves.

Little Grey is watching. He is sure he can do
this too, but when he tries he is bowled
over and over by the rush and swell.
Startled, he heads away, pulsing
his distress. Old Grey swerves
in her course just enough to lift
Little Grey up to the air. He blows
an agitated plume of bubbles and water
before they dive again.

OLD GREY KEEPS CLOSE to the coast as
she travels. She is listening to the Pacific Ocean,
the varying temperature of the water, the strength
of the currents, the taste and smell and feel of the
ebb and flow against her skin. Suddenly Little Grey
starts. This is nothing he knows – a regular
thumping shuddering juddering metallic sound.

Old Grey swerves. She has heard boat engines often, but always

coming from a distance so she can avoid them. This one has

burst into roaring frenzy close… dangerously close!

A ship's engineer has just finished working

on a faulty engine. She and Little Grey dive deep.

THE SEA TASTES OILY, and the vibrations shocking down from above grow stronger and stronger. Old Grey knows Little Grey is panicking. He needs to breathe to get away. With one mighty heave of her tail she pushes them out beyond the immediate throb of the motor and they burst up to the surface of the water and blow high into the air. Behind them on the deck of the Los Angeles pleasure boat there is consternation.

"Whales! Whales! Cut the engines! Now! Hurry!"

The thumping stops as suddenly as it had begun. Little Grey blows again and again, and then feeds from his mother for comfort. Old Grey keeps them moving, but slowly now, and the boat is left behind.

APRIL ENDS AND MAY BEGINS.

The sea is getting colder, but Little Grey
is fat and rounded from his mother's milk,
and well protected from the chilly waters.
He is bolder now, and frisks and swirls
about Old Grey while she swims steadily
on and on. She has eaten very little since
she left the Arctic five months before;
she is thinner by far, and needs to save
her strength.

The land is long and low on her right-hand
side; from time to time she surges up to look
around, her huge head a shining mountain
rising from the waves. Little Grey tries
to spy hop too, but he finds himself sliding
back into the water too quickly to see
more than a glimmer of the shoreline.

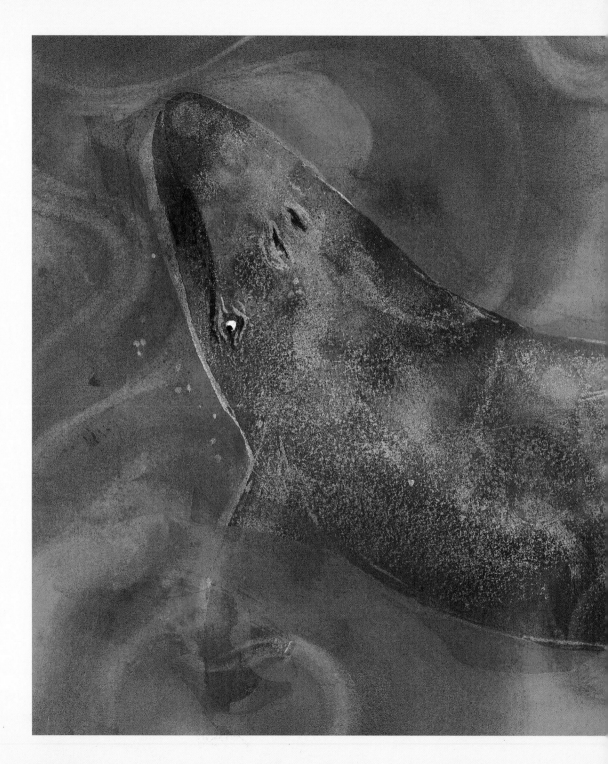

THE ORCAS come from nowhere.
Sleek black and white shadows, all at once
they surround Little Grey. Already blood
is clouding the water. Little Grey
is clicking and pulsing and twisting and
turning, his tail flukes streaming red.

Pain is tearing into him, but he cannot
tell where to go. Orcas are everywhere
he looks, scything in front of him, slicing
down behind him... Where is his mother?

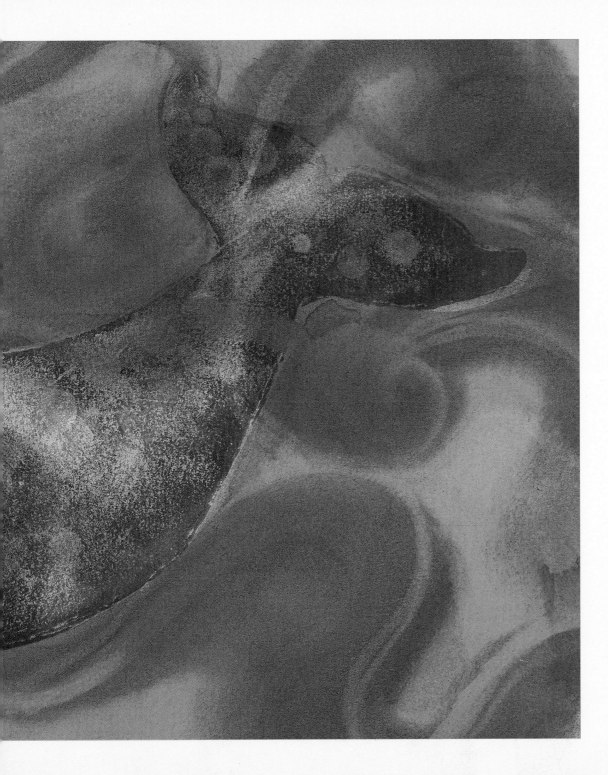

Old Grey turns, fear for her little one driving her into a terrible anger. She launches herself at the killer whales, trying desperately to put her massive body between them and Little Grey. But there are too many of them. She thrashes with her mighty tail, but still they come, and she cannot see Little Grey for the clouds of blood around him. She can only sense his soundless screaming…

THERE IS A SWIRL, and a vast grey shape slides between Little Grey and the Orcas. It is Three Scars. She pushes Little Grey towards his mother; he is held safe between them. The Orcas, angry at the sudden disappearance of their prey,

tear into the newcomer, ripping at her tail and at her lips and tongue. To Three Scars it is almost as if they do not exist. She moves in total harmony with Old Grey, taking Little Grey to shallower waters where the kelp beds offer safety. The Orcas do not wish to follow.

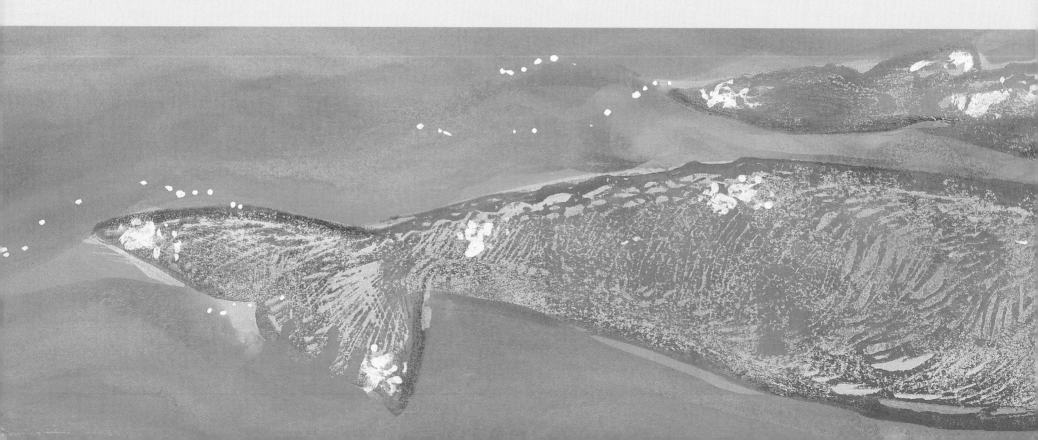

Three Scars, Old Grey and Little Grey
stay among the sheltering seaweed
for some time. Little Grey mends
quickly, but his tail flukes
will be scarred for ever.
Three Scars is slower to heal;
her tongue is badly torn
and swollen.

Old Grey swims by her side
encouraging her, sometimes gently
nudging her. Little Grey keeps close
to his mother, no longer splashing
and playing. They travel on,
more slowly now,
but steadily.

MAY IS NEARLY OVER when Old Grey and Little Grey reach the Bering Straits. The Northern sun is pale, but the days are long and light.

Three Scars is swimming heavily and wearily, but as she feels the swell of the icy cold water even she climbs and dives with a stronger heave of her huge, tired body. Maybe she will never make the journey south again...

There will be good food in the Arctic waters, and time to rest and recover. Already Old Grey is diving down to scrape her path in the ocean floor, filling her vast, cavernous mouth with krill and thousands and thousands of tiny sea creatures.

THE END OF MAY. At last they arrive, through the Bering Straits and into the Chukchi Sea. . . their home for the summer, where they will feed and grow fat and strong.

Little Grey is filled with a wild excitement. This is a new place, a cold place, a strange place, but with sea waters rich with food. He dives below Three Scars, and rolls and twists as he comes up again. He has made his first ever journey to the North!

He blows a triumphant spout, and a rainbow plays over the water as he dives again.

For dear Gabby and Flynn
with much love – **V.F.**

For Elaine Flather – **L.F.**

Copyright © 1998 Zero to Ten Limited
Text copyright © 1998 Vivian French
Illustrations copyright © 1998 Lisa Flather

Publisher: Anna McQuinn
Art Director: Tim Foster
Senior Art Editor: Sarah Godwin
Designer: Tiffany Leeson
Senior Editor: Rebecca Orr Deas

First published in Great Britain in 1998
by Zero to Ten Limited
46 Chalvey Road East, Slough, Berkshire SL1 2LR

A CIP catalogue record for this book
is available from the British Library.

ISBN 1-84089-077-0

Printed in Hong Kong